Illustrated by Alan Brown

Rourke
Educational Media
rourkeeducationalmedia.com

www.rourkeeducationalmedia.com

Edited by: Keli Sipperley
Cover and Interior layout by: Rhea Magaro-Wallace
Cover and Interior Illustrations by: Alan Brown

Library of Congress PCN Data

Runaway Robot / J.L. Anderson
 (Paisley Atoms)
 ISBN (hard cover)(alk. paper) 978-1-68191-716-0
 ISBN (soft cover) 978-1-68191-817-4
 ISBN (e-Book) 978-1-68191-912-6
 Library of Congress Control Number: 2016932593

Printed in the United States of America,
North Mankato, Minnesota

Dear Parents and Teachers,

Future world-famous scientist Paisley Atoms and her best friend, Ben Striker, aren't afraid to stir things up in their quests for discovery. Using Paisley's basement as a laboratory, the two are constantly inventing, exploring, and, well, making messes. Paisley has a few bruises to show for their work, too. She wears them like badges of honor.

These fast-paced adventures weave fascinating facts, quotes from real scientists, and explanations for various phenomena into witty dialogue, stealthily boosting your reader's understanding of multiple science topics. From sound waves to dinosaurs, from the sea floor to the moon, Paisley, Ben and the gang are perfect partner resources for a STEAM curriculum.

Each illustrated chapter book includes a science experiment or activity, a biography of a woman in science, jokes, and websites to visit.

In addition, each book also includes online teacher/parent notes with ideas for incorporating the story into a lesson plan. These notes include subject matter, background information, inspiration for maker space activities, comprehension questions, and additional online resources. Notes are available at: www.RourkeEducationalMedia.com.

We hope you enjoy Paisley and her pals as much as we do.

Happy reading,
Rourke Educational Media

Table of Contents

CHAPTER ONE
Building a Robot

Paisley Atoms tripped over a box as she walked into her house after school. It had *PERISHABLE* and *LIVE ANIMALS* labels all over it. "You think Mom sent us a pet from Mexico?" she asked her best friend, Ben Striker.

Paisley's mom was researching plant species in Mexico and had sent them a few treats before, plus stacks of field notes and plant specimens. She'd even mailed some Mexican garden decorations.

Newton, the Atoms' rescued pet mongoose, crouched low to sniff the new mystery box.

"Based on the size and shape of the box, I think we can safely say it isn't a jaguar," Ben said.

Newton chattered.

"Don't worry, Newton, we'll love you even if we get a new pet," Paisley said.

Paisley opened the box with Ben's help.

"Looks like some kind of insect," Ben said. He loved insects. He especially loved to watch his harvester ant collection. They worked hard and were so organized.

"They're beetles. Thousands and thousands and thousands of beetles," Paisley said, checking out the Dermestid Beetle Colony kit.

Flour dust clouded the air as Dad walked out of the kitchen. Paisley could only imagine what the kitchen looked like at the moment.

"Hey, you two," Dad said. "Hope school went well. Oh good! My flesh-eating beetles arrived." He broke into his happy air-guitar dance. Dad was the only person Paisley could think of that would dance for bugs. Well, other than Ben.

Paisley studied the beetles. "Flesh-eating beetles, huh?" They didn't have fangs or look bloodthirsty or anything. Newton licked his lips.

"Don't even think about eating them," Dad said to Newton. "These beetles will be doing some important work for me."

"They don't bite, do they?" Paisley asked.

"Not humans. They don't carry any diseases either. They'll naturally clean some bones," Dad said. His office overflowed with lots of strange stuff these days, including a deep freezer with parts of a bison skeleton. He was working extra hours to put on an American Grasslands display at the university.

Ben watched the beetles and their larvae so long, Paisley had to tug on his arm to pull him away. "Still want to run some experiments in the lab?" she asked.

Ben hesitated, then followed Paisley. She tripped over one of Newton's squeaky toys as they squeezed through a hallway lined with overgrown plants to get to their basement lab.

The place was a mess.

"Too bad my dad couldn't use a robot to clean the bones instead of beetles," Paisley said. The house was already a disaster without the addition of the freezer full of bones, and now, Dermestid beetles.

"Flesh-eating robots could turn into a nightmare if they don't get programmed right," Ben said. He pretended he was getting attacked.

Paisley laughed. "I didn't think that all the way through. We could at least use a robot to help with our chores. The place is a wreck."

"I can't believe I've let things get so disorganized," Ben said. He took after his neat parents and was usually orderly like his ants.

Paisley looked around their lab. They had safety goggles, a couple of fire extinguishers, multi-meters, different types of scopes, beakers, batteries, art supplies, recycled materials, plus a bunch of other stuff scattered about. Newton had even shredded a large poster board to build himself a makeshift den.

Ben stared at a printer and scanner combo. Coils and wires stuck out of the machine like hay from a scarecrow's head. "A robot would be awesome! Millions of robots are used all over the world to build industrial stuff. Surely we could design one to help with chores."

"As long as we don't come up with some sort of flesh-eating robot that tries to attack us, our lives will be much simpler," Paisley said.

She told Ben about an article she'd read about a woman named Melonee Wise who designed robots. "Melonee Wise and her team built a robot called UBR-1 to do all kinds of stuff around the house, like get drinks and clean out the dishwasher."

"Talk about living up to your last name," Ben said.

"No kidding," Paisley said, though she liked her last name and Ben's, too. *Atoms and Striker* had a nice ring to it if they decided to start their own robotics company one day.

"My parents were talking about how kids born today might not ever drive a car because of robotics," Ben said. "I hope that one doesn't pan out."

Paisley liked the idea of driving a car someday

as well. If not, maybe they could dream up a driving adventure together using the ancient key her mom had given her.

"We should build a semi-humanoid robot like UBR-1 that can do our chores and more," Ben said.

Paisley liked the sound of that. "Chores and More actually makes a good robot name."

"Let's build the robot first and then decide on a name," he said.

"True." Paisley loved the possibility of never having to do chores again. "We should start with a robot base and body."

Paisley and Ben dug their way through their lab, but didn't find anything large enough that could do stuff like sweep, scrub the toilets, and mop the kitchen.

"We could use that box the beetles came in," Ben said. He told her about a video he saw of a man who turned a cardboard box into a pet robot on wheels.

Paisley liked that idea until she caught Newton chewing up some more poster board a second later. "Newton! No more paper for you!"

"On second thought, we might need something sturdier," Ben said.

"How about a vacuum?" Paisley said. It wasn't like the vacuum in the coat closet upstairs was getting much use these days.

"Eureka!" Ben said.

When they went to grab the vacuum, they saw Dad setting up a big chamber for the beetles to clean off the bison bones. He could barely move around in his office.

After, they went into the kitchen for an apple snack. The countertops and floor were dusted in flour. Paisley might've been annoyed with the mess, but at least it meant that Dad was making one of her favorite things: sweet potato biscuits with cumin and chili.

"I can't wait for dinner," Ben said, chomping on the apple. He was always hungry these days.

Newton gobbled up some mealworms.

Paisley's hands were sticky, and when she washed them off in the kitchen sink, she found an arm for the robot in the dish strainer: a spatula.

"How about barbeque tongs for the other arm?" Ben asked.

Yes! The robot was coming together. They continued working in the kitchen and attached a flashlight with duct tape to the top of the vacuum for the robot's

heart. They used the printer and scanner combo for the abdomen.

"What should we use for the head?" Ben asked. He added a couple of extra pieces of duct tape for good measure.

Paisley remembered a particular garden decoration her mom had sent. "I think we can find the head outside," Paisley said as they walked past Dad's office.

Dad looked up right as he set the bison head into the beetle cleaning chamber. "I need to pick up some more supplies before dinner, so call me if you need anything before then," he said.

Life was interesting in the Atoms family.

CHAPTER TWO
Chores and More?

Dad waved at Paisley and Ben before he left.

The next-door neighbors, Mrs. Pendlebury and her young daughter, Mia, were pruning some shrubs, which already looked perfect when Paisley and Ben went outside. They waved, but only Mia waved back.

"Can I go play with Paisley?" Mia asked.

"I'm afraid you'll get lost in the Atoms' jungle of a front yard," Mrs. Pendlebury said.

Paisley scowled. When Mom was home, their yard looked amazing, even if she let the native species grow out from time to time so the plants would go to seed.

Everything had grown out these days.

"Your family should really take better care of your property," Mrs. Pendlebury said. "I hope the inside of your house isn't as junky as the outside."

Ben rolled his eyes, and Paisley fought to keep herself from saying something rude. "We're taking care of it," Paisley said.

Mia jumped up. "I can help you!"

Mrs. Pendlebury shook her head. "You can help me by straightening out the garden path lights you knocked over."

"Mrs. Pendlebury would freak out if she knew about the bones and the beetles inside," Paisley whispered to Ben. "I bet she wouldn't approve of Newton either."

Ben laughed. Together, they moved overgrown plants out of the way to find the beautiful garden decoration Mom had sent. The colorful Talavera garden sphere came from Puebla, Mexico, and it would make a wonderful robot head.

Paisley picked it up and carried it inside to where the robot was set up in the kitchen. Mom wouldn't be

too pleased, but they cut a small hole in the bottom of the pottery so it could pop on the handle of the vacuum. All it did was sit and look pretty in the garden, anyway.

"Our robot looks complete now," Paisley said.

Ben stood back to admire it. "We just need to figure out how to power it."

Newton sniffed their creation, but seemed less impressed. Paisley and Ben tried to plug the vacuum in, but the robot didn't come to life. Not that they really expected it to be that easy.

"Let's put the key near the flashlight heart," Ben suggested.

"I was thinking the same thing," Paisley said. The ancient key contained power from the past and energized their adventures.

"Please come to life as a robot so we can clean up," Paisley said.

She bumped her fist with Ben's. "Science Alliance!" they yelled.

Their robot still didn't come to life.

"We're missing something," Paisley said.

"Eyes and ears," Ben said.

Paisley thought about the Pendlebury's garden path lights outside. "We could borrow the solar cells to make eyes and ears. They'd even give our robot a power boost."

"Be that as it may, I don't think Mrs. Pendlebury will like the idea," Ben said.

"No kidding. Maybe she doesn't have to know. We can build our robot, tidy up, and then return the solar cells before she notices they're gone," Paisley said.

Ben adjusted his glasses and flipped through his field notebook while he thought about it.

"Come on, Ben. It's not like we'd be stealing them or anything. If Mrs. Pendlebury is still outside, I'll ask for permission," Paisley said.

Ben paused for a moment longer and doodled what he thought their robot would look like with solar cells for eyes and ears. "Okay, let's go."

As Paisley twisted the front door open, she really hoped Mrs. Pendlebury had gone back inside with Mia. "We'll be right back, Newton."

"The coast is clear," Ben said.

"Whew," she whispered, even though Mrs. Pendlebury's car was gone and she was nowhere in sight.

Paisley's hands shook as she popped out four solar cells from the garden path lights with Ben's help. She reminded herself that they were just borrowing them and not breaking anything or stealing.

When they got back inside the Atoms' house, they used double-sided tape to stick on the solar cells for the robot's eyes and ears. It really did seem more complete.

Paisley pressed the key up against the robot's flashlight heart again. "Science Alliance!" they repeated.

The vacuum hummed to life even though they hadn't plugged it in. The flashlight flipped on automatically and the solar cells glowed. Newton jumped back and chirped.

"So nice to meet you, Chores and More," Paisley said to the robot.

The robot held up the spatula arm. Paisley shook it first, then Ben. He stared at their creation for a moment in disbelief before adding a few more details in his journal.

Paisley wasn't sure what to ask of their robot first. Maybe they should just go room by room. "Will you help clean the kitchen?" she asked the robot.

The solar cells flickered as if their robot understood, but then it didn't do anything.

"Maybe we should show the robot what to do first," Ben said.

Again, the robot's solar cells flickered. Paisley grabbed a washcloth and showed the robot how to wipe down the flour-dusted countertops. Ben swept up crumbs from the floor.

"See what we're doing?" Paisley asked the robot. "Can you try it now?"

She set the washcloth over the robot's spatula arm and Ben set the broom in the tong hands, wrapping a piece of cloth around it to hold it in place.

The robot moved forward about a foot and rotated its arms. Yes! This was the moment the two of them had been waiting for. Sure, they would need to return

the solar cells at some point, but they would find a replacement soon. Chores were going to be a thing of the past!

But Chores and More stopped moving and rotated its pottery head as if confused.

"Maybe we need to show you what to do again," Paisley said.

The countertops sparkled by the time Paisley finished her wiping demonstration. The floors were mostly free of crumbs after Ben's example.

"At this rate, we might as well do all of the cleaning ourselves," Paisley said.

CHAPTER THREE
Talavera Gets to Work

"If at first you don't succeed, try a different experiment," Ben said.

"Have any ideas?" Paisley asked.

"Please help us clean," Ben asked the robot in Japanese. At least he tried to, since he was just starting to learn the language.

Chores and More moved forward a couple of feet, sucking up some of the bits and pieces on the floor.

Ben was onto something, so Paisley asked for help, this time in Spanish. The robot moved forward another couple of feet.

Sure, the path was better than it was before, but the kitchen was now mostly clean thanks to old-fashioned human effort.

"Science is a way of thinking," Ben said, quoting Carl Sagan, an astronomer just like the man Ben was named after, Benjamin Banneker.

"We need to think this through some more," Paisley said. After a moment, she came up with an idea. "How about we take Chores and More into the hallway to see if a change in the environment makes a difference?"

Paisley and Ben carefully moved their robot into the hallway. The robot swiveled its head. Newton pounced on the robot's unplugged vacuum cord.

"Can you help clean up this clutter?" Paisley asked.

The robot still seemed clueless. Or maybe it was just lazy. Ben tried out several other languages including Italian, German, and French.

Meanwhile, Paisley modeled what she wanted the robot to do by putting items back in their proper places. Newton ran circles around her. The hallway was far less crowded when Paisley had another idea.

"Maybe you don't like your name!" she said. "How about we name you after the pottery you're made of? Do you like Talavera better?"

The robot's solar cells sparkled.

"I think that means yes," Ben said. "Our robot decided on a name for itself."

"Ok, then, Talavera," Paisley said. She talked to the robot while continuing to do her own chores, sharing details about her friends at school like Arjun, the twins Suki and Sumi, Rosalind, and even her nemesis, Whitney-Raelynn.

Newton chattered as if trying to communicate with the robot, too.

"Newton was rescued from India when he was injured as a baby," Paisley said.

Ben gave up on the languages and drew a couple of things in his notebook. He drew a big X on the page since his ideas failed.

Talavera swiveled around to see it. The solar cells flashed.

"That was strange," Paisley said. "Try writing down

another letter."

Ben wrote down Y next since it came after X. Talavera's arms flailed and it moved the remaining boxes out of the hall. Finally, their robot was doing some work!

When Ben wrote down the letter Z in the notebook, Talavera cleared the remaining items in the hallway and vacuumed the floor perfectly.

"X, Y, Z. Our robot must like the alphabet," Paisley said to Ben.

"Alphabet!" Ben said. "I get it now."

"Can you fill me in?" Paisley asked over the hum of the vacuum. Talavera was doing an amazing job cleaning—finally!

"Chi, Psi, Zeta," Ben said.

It sounded like he was talking about some of the Greek houses around Dad's university. Then it all started to make sense to Paisley! Those were Greek letters used in math, science, and engineering.

"Write down more, Ben, and show Talavera," Paisley said.

Ben had to race to catch up to their robot. He wrote down a few more symbols. "Beta, Delta, and Pi."

Talavera roared to life and went room to room. Paisley and Ben stood back in awe as their robot scrubbed, mopped, sorted, organized, washed, and dried until the place looked orderly like Ben's harvester ant collection.

Newton followed the robot throughout the whole house as if it was the best game ever. Paisley closed Dad's office door so nothing would happen to the bones or the beetles.

Paisley and Ben did their math homework while the robot took care of their basement lab. This might've been their best creation yet.

"Robots really do make life easier," Paisley said.

When the house looked so good that even Mrs. Pendlebury would approve, minus the bison bones and beetles, they all took a break.

Newton climbed up the robot's shoulder. Talavera's eyes glowed softly.

"I think the robot likes you," Paisley said. "Ben, I'm not so sure I can return the solar cells."

"We have to. The agreement was that we were just going to borrow them," Ben said.

Paisley nodded. For now, they still had some time to get some other things done.

"We should clean up the yard," Paisley said. "Mrs. Pendlebury kind of had a point and it would make Mom happy. She's going to go on and on about how good everything looks when I video chat with her later." Paisley's dad would be really surprised when he came home from his errand!

Newton followed them outside and checked out the garden decorations.

Ben wrote down some random Greek symbols. "Kappa, Nu, Omega."

The base of their robot might've been a vacuum, but the power from the key, the solar cells, and the symbols helped it to suck up the grass like a lawnmower. The robot's tongs plucked the weeds and pruned the shrubs.

Just watching the robot do all the work felt wrong, so Paisley and Ben pitched in. They tossed some piles of weeds at each other as Mrs. Pendlebury's car pulled up.

"Good," Mrs. Pendlebury said to them after she parked in her driveway. "The place looks a touch more acceptable."

"How cute," Mia said as she spotted Newton romping in the much-shorter grass.

"What is that weasel doing in your yard?" Mrs. Pendlebury asked. "And what is that thing?" She scowled when she saw Talavera.

Talavera's eyes dimmed. Would Mrs. Pendlebury realize that those were the solar cells from her very own yard that they borrowed without permission?

Paisley scooped Newton up for Mia to see and prepared to educate Mrs. Pendlebury about mongooses.

"Mia, you better get inside before you get bit or get weasel fleas," Mrs. Pendlebury said. She marched Mia inside the house, pausing right by the garden path lights with the missing solar cells.

How much trouble would Mrs. Pendlebury cause if she noticed them?

Paisley held her breath.

CHAPTER FOUR
Fire!

Maybe she was too busy trying to keep Mia from getting "weasel fleas," or maybe the sun had lowered enough in the sky that Mrs. Pendlebury didn't notice that her lights had been tampered with.

Paisley exhaled. Ben breathed out even louder.

"Mia Pendlebury, you get in this house right this minute!" her mother yelled.

Mia obeyed, right after she scratched Newton's head. He only nipped fingers if he felt threatened, but he liked the little girl's attention. Mia then patted Talavera on the head before running inside.

"You better wash your hands several times," Mrs. Pendlebury said to Mia.

"That was a close call," Ben said once they were in the house. "I think we should go inside, too."

Paisley didn't want to take any other chances. Talavera and Newton followed them into the living room. Other than Dad's office, which was still closed off, the place looked spotless and more organized than ever. Paisley didn't want to return the solar cells. They could get a replacement, but would it change Talavera somehow? An agreement was an agreement, though.

Ben grabbed his math textbook and homework. Talavera's eyes and ears dimmed again. The solar power seemed to be drooping with all of the robot's work and, since the sun was setting, it reduced the solar energy.

"Before we say goodbye, I want to check something

out. If our robot responds to Greek symbols, how would it respond to actual math problems?" Ben asked.

After looking at the math textbook, their robot hummed louder. The scanner portion of its abdomen glowed bright green. The unit hadn't worked in so long that Paisley wasn't sure what it normally looked like.

Suddenly, the glow decreased and the solar cells dimmed again. "Are you okay?" she asked the robot.

The robot used the tongs to grab the textbook and pulled it near the scanner bed.

"It's like Talavera is thinking," Paisley whispered to Ben.

The "insert paper" button on the printer glowed red before it started to fade to orange.

Ben wrote out "Theta" and "Gamma." The Greek letters didn't have any effect this time.

Ben tried a couple more letters, but their robot seemed to be fading just like the solar cells. "Please hang in there, Talavera," Ben said. "Pretty please."

Paisley wasn't sure how much the robot could understand, but Ben's begging seemed to fuel it. The light turned red again. The insert button blinked like it was waiting for them to respond.

"I can't believe this," Paisley whispered as she scrambled to find paper. It was stacked in such a neat pile on the desk she couldn't find it at first. When she finally found it, she loaded a stack into the robot's printer belly.

The printer hummed to life. Paisley wasn't sure what was going to happen, but then a page printed out.

"It's the answers to our math homework," Paisley said. She compared the robot's answer to those she and Ben had come up with earlier. They were identical.

Even their strict math teacher, Mr. Rhombus, would've been impressed with the correct fraction multiplications. He would not be impressed if they cheated, though.

Paisley had been friends with Ben for so long it was like he could read her mind sometimes.

"We can just use this to double-check our answers," Ben said. "We usually have the answers right anyway. It will save us a lot of busy work if we're ever in a pinch."

Paisley stared at the paper. It felt a little warm in

her hands, but maybe that was just her imagination. Or perhaps it was guilt making her think that.

Page after page of the math answers printed out. The time they saved could give them more time in the lab, which is where they did their best learning anyway. Then she thought of how the kids at her school like Arjun, Rosalind, Suki, and Sumi would react. Their nemesis, Whitney-Raelynn, would hold it over their heads forever.

"You were the one worrying about 'borrowing' the solar cells earlier," Paisley said.

"You made a good argument about returning them," Ben said.

"We can't exactly return the answers once we have them," Paisley said. "You're getting a little carried away, Ben."

Ben wasn't the only one getting carried away. Talavera printed out pages so quickly that a wisp of smoke rose up from the printer unit.

"It's okay, you can stop, Talavera," said Paisley.

The robot didn't listen. More smoke spilled out of

the printer and there was a small red glow. This time, it wasn't the printer button.

Newton screeched.

"Fire!" Paisley and Ben yelled at the same time.

The closest fire extinguishers were in Dad's office. Paisley opened the door and rushed inside.

"The wall!" Ben said, pointing to two extinguishers sitting on a shelf.

Paisley wasn't sure which one to grab until she saw the sign "Dry Chemical Fire Extinguisher." They would need that to put out an electronics fire.

"PASS," Ben said to Paisley as she reached up to grab it. That was what Dad had taught them about using an extinguisher if a fire broke out.

P was for *pull the handle*. Paisley pulled the pin on the handle.

A was for *aim the extinguisher*. Paisley aimed it at the middle of the robot's belly.

S was for *squeeze*. She squeezed the lever slowly. A cloud of white shot out.

S was for *sweep*. Paisley held the nozzle to sweep at

the base of the fire.

The flames disappeared. The smell of the smoke lingered in the air.

"Good work fighting that blaze," Ben said.

Talavera's eyes and ears were now dark. It was motionless.

"I think we lost our robot," Paisley whispered.

Ben checked to make sure the fire was out. The white cloud from the fire extinguisher settled on the ground and all over. His shoes left imprints in the white residue.

"I feel horrible. I don't know what got into me," Ben said. Then he grabbed Talavera's spatula arm to see if he could feel a pulse or some sign of life. Of course he couldn't feel a pulse because it wasn't created to have one. The robot didn't have blood flowing through any veins.

"The place looks amazing, but what's that smell?" Dad asked as he walked into the house.

"We had some parts overheat," Ben said. "Paisley took care of it before anything bad happened."

As soon as the words were out of his mouth, that's exactly when something bad went down.

CHAPTER FIVE
Hole in the Wall

Talavera's eyes and ears strobed and the robot swiveled around before zooming around in a large circle. Grass clippings spilled from the robot's vacuum bag. All the cleaning was being undone in a matter of minutes.

"What's going on?" Dad asked.

Paisley filled him in about how they made the

robot and borrowed a few objects without asking.

Dad might've started to lecture them, but Talavera's arms flapped up and down. The robot shrieked and raced into Dad's office.

"NOOOOooooo!" Dad yelled as Talavera flipped over the container with the bones and the Dermestid beetles.

The bones flew everywhere while the beetles scattered all over the floor. The carpet looked like a living archaeological site.

Newton was either rounding the beetles up or having a feast. Before Paisley could decide, the robot blasted a hole in the wall.

The robot shoved bricks aside and pushed all the way through, leaving a gaping hole behind it as it sped off into the yard.

"We have a runaway robot!" Ben shouted.

What if Mia was outside? Would the robot try to hurt her or her family members? The robot had tongs for arms and was incredibly strong.

"We have to stop Talavera!" Paisley cried.

Paisley, Ben, and Dad bolted through the hole in the wall to chase the robot down. A trail of the beetles followed them.

At the speed the robot was going, it could've exploded through the walls of Roarington Elementary in no time. Their school might have been old, but it was good and had lots of expensive equipment.

Talavera didn't get that far, though. It stopped in the Pendlebury's yard. Like some kind of scene from a horror movie, the robot used its arms to pop off its pottery head.

The head flopped off of the vacuum's base and thudded onto the ground. It rolled near the Pendlebury's garden area. Dad stood there in disbelief.

"What do you think is happening?" Ben asked.

The solar cells flickered on and then off. On and then off.

"I think the power wants to be returned to the garden path lights," Paisley said.

"I never should've pressed things," Ben said.

"Me neither," Paisley said. She reached for the key

around her neck. Even though their robot experiment had gone awry, Paisley still hesitated to let it go. After a moment, she pressed the key against the solar panel. "Please go back to your normal state. Goodbye Talavera," Paisley said.

Dad inspected the pottery while Paisley and Ben put the solar cells back where they belonged. "I hope you two have learned an important lesson," Dad said.

"Oh, we've learned a lot," Paisley said. "To start with, we should've asked for permission."

Right at that moment, Mrs. Pendlebury stormed out of the front door. Mia clung to her leg. "Speaking of permission, who gave you permission to mess around in my garden?"

Mia moved over to look at the tumbled vacuum base and picked up the spatula that had fallen off.

"And don't touch that thing!" Mrs. Pendlebury said.

"Mom!" Mia said. "This won't have any fleas."

Paisley wanted to run inside the robot-shaped hole in the wall of her house to avoid having to apologize to Mrs. Pendlebury. They needed to make things right, though. "I'm really sorry about the mess. I borrowed some of the solar cells from these lights without your permission." She wasn't sure what to say about their robot experiment since their neighbor frowned on things like that—and most everything about the Atoms family.

Ben spoke up. "We borrowed them to make improvements, but we made a few things worse."

That's when Mrs. Pendlebury gasped as she looked at the hole in her neighbor's house. Good thing she didn't see the bison bones on the floor of Dad's strange, messy office. She might've even passed out if she saw the long line of Dermestid beetles crawling into her yard.

At least they wouldn't bite anyone. And if there were any bones in the Pendleburys' yard, they would be cleaned in a day or two, depending on how hungry the beetles were.

"Don't worry, we'll fix it up as good as new soon," Paisley said. She wasn't sure how, but they would figure out a way. "We will make things up to you by volunteering to do your yard work."

Paisley thought about building a robot with a non-borrowed power source to do the work for them, but for now, she actually didn't mind doing chores the old fashioned way.

"We're sorry," Ben said.

Mrs. Pendlebury's face got so red that Paisley thought she might've started screaming and shouting at them. Could Paisley blame her?

"I forgive you both. Thanks for apologizing and for being a good role model for Mia ... mostly," Mrs. Pendlebury said in a calm voice.

Paisley could hardly believe Mrs. Pendlebury would say that!

"How about you help us plant some new shrubs this weekend? It will help us block out an eyesore," Mrs. Pendlebury said, her eyes wandering over to the Atoms' home.

Just when Paisley was starting to warm up to their neighbor! "We'll be there bright and early on Saturday," Paisley said, forcing a smile. "I'll see to it that we keep the place tidier from here on out." She showed she meant it by collecting the parts that once made up Talavera. Ben put the pottery sphere back in the Atoms' front garden where they'd found it.

Mrs. Pendlebury seemed satisfied with that. Now the question remained as to how Paisley could make things up to her parents.

"Sorry" always was a good start and Paisley really meant it when she said it. Ben apologized, too.

"You are grounded for two weeks except to help Mrs. Pendlebury," Dad said as they walked back inside.

Paisley groaned.

"It would've been a month, but I was thinking about expanding my office anyway," Dad said. "I'm not pleased with everything that happened, but I am impressed you two built such a dynamic robot. The place really looks good minus a few major details," he added.

"We'll clean it up," Paisley promised.

Paisley and Ben decided to keep the math homework

aspect of their adventure to themselves. For now, at least. They also volunteered to give up their allowance for a while to cover the costs of fixing things. Hopefully Mom would handle the situation as well as Dad, all things considered. Paisley would have to wait until she talked to her later.

Together, Paisley, Ben, and Dad checked out the office. Newton was asleep on Dad's chair. The busy day seemed to have caught up with him, or perhaps he had a belly full of beetles.

The bison bones were surprisingly clean and some of the remaining beetles were easy enough to round up. "It'll take a while to build the colony of beetles back up, but I can return the bones to the university. I think this is a sign I should take less work projects home with me," Dad said.

Paisley thought that was a good idea.

Ben's stomach grumbled and soon they'd eat some of the sweet potato biscuits with cumin and chili.

While they waited for dinner, Paisley and Ben threw away all of the pages with the math answers. It was a lot more enjoyable working on their homework without any fiery assistance.

Science Alliance!
Program a Friend

Robots must be programmed before they can perform. During the programming phase, errors can happen easily. Programmers keep testing and retesting until they find and fix all of the problems. Here is an activity where you can build a fun obstacle course with your friends and then try to "program" your friends to avoid hitting any of the obstacles.

Materials:
* large space (indoor or outdoor)
* obstacles like balls, boxes, pillows, other toys, etc.
* blindfold
* paper and pencil

Step 1
Make sure to clear an outdoor or indoor space.

Step 2

Set out the obstacles to create a maze.

Step 3

Blindfold your friend and give them specific steps that tell them how to get through the maze. The goal is to not hit any of the obstacles.

Step 4

Make corrections as your friend moves.

Step 5

Write down all of the steps it would take for your friend to get through the maze.

Step 6

Give the written steps to your friend to make it through the maze. If your friend hits anything, they have to start all over!

Women in Science

Robots can be used for things such as space exploration, military missions, industrial manufacturing, construction, and for entertainment like toys and programmable pets. Melonee Wise designs, builds, and programs robotic hardware. She is known for her work building the world's most sophisticated personal robot. Dr. Cynthia Breazeal has made many recent social robotics breakthroughs in her work at the Massachusetts Institute of Technology, where she is the director of the Personal Robots Group at the MIT Media Laboratory.

Melonee Wise

Dr. Cynthia Breazeai

Author Q & A

Q: How did you get the idea for this story?

A: My husband is an engineer and the two of us had a blast brainstorming ideas on a long road trip.

Q: What chore do you wish a robot could do for you?

A: Hmm...any sort of housework so that I can spend more time writing.

Q: Have you ever "borrowed" something like Paisley?

A: Yes, and I felt really bad when I broke my brother's "borrowed" game.

Silly Science!

Q: **When does a robot need to get some training?**

A: Whenever it gets rusty!

Q: **Does a robot have a favorite type of music?**

A: Of course—heavy metal.

Q: **Is it possible for a robot to get mad?**

A: Yes, if someone pushes its buttons.

Websites to Visit

Robotics and engineer project ideas:

www.sciencebuddies.org/
  science-fair-projects/Intro-Robotics.shtml

How to make your own mini-robot:

www.redtedart.com/2011/12/30/
  how-to-make-a-mini-robot

All about robots:

www.galileo.org/robotics

About the Author

J.L. Anderson's education inspired her to become an author, but she thought seriously about becoming a biologist, and she once was the president of the science club in high school. She lives outside of Austin, Texas with her husband, daughter, and two naughty dogs. You can learn more about her at www.jessicaleeanderson.com.

About the Illustrator

Alan Brown's love of comic art, cartoons and drawing has driven him to follow his dreams of becoming an artist. His career as a freelance artist and designer has allowed him to work on a wide range of projects, from magazine illustration and game design to children's books. He's had the good fortune to work on comics such as *Ben 10* and *Bravest Warriors*. Alan lives in Newcastle with his wife, sons and dog.